Search for the Sea Monster

Ahoy, mateys!

Set sail for a brand-new
adventure with the

#1 *Stowaway!*
#2 *X Marks the Spot*
#3 *Catnapped!*
#4 *Sea Sick*
Super Special #1 *Ghost Ship*
#5 *Search for the Sea Monster*

Coming Soon:
Super Special #2 *Best in Class*

Search for the Sea Monster

by Erin Soderberg
illustrations by Russ Cox

A STEPPING STONE BOOK™
Random House New York

For Wally, my goofy, adventurous,
and very huggable pup

 Published in the United States by Random House Children's Books, a division of Penguin Random House LLC, New York.

Random House and the colophon are registered trademarks and A Stepping Stone Book and the colophon are trademarks of Penguin Random House LLC.

Visit us on the Web!
SteppingStonesBooks.com
randomhousekids.com

Educators and librarians, for a variety of teaching tools, visit us at
RHTeachersLibrarians.com

Library of Congress Cataloging-in-Publication Data is available upon request.

ISBN 978-1-101-93776-1 (trade) — ISBN 978-1-101-93777-8 (lib. bdg.) —
ISBN 978-1-101-93778-5 (ebook)

Printed in the United States of America
10 9 8 7 6 5 4

This book has been officially leveled by using the F&P Text Level Gradient™ Leveling System.

Random House Children's Books supports the First Amendment and celebrates the right to read.

CONTENTS

1. Noisy Naptime........................ 1

2. Don't Spook the Little Guy.......... 8

3. Who Said Monster?.................... 17

4. Too Many Cats in the Sea............ 24

5. Slime Trail.......................... 32

6. The Search for Slime................ 42

7. The Sea Slug......................... 52

8. The Battle Begins................... 60

9. Not Tough Enough.................... 68

10. Little Einstein's Big Idea......... 77

Noisy Naptime

Wally the puppy pirate loved naps almost as much as he loved meaty snacks and belly rubs. The fluffy golden retriever stretched his hind legs and yawned. He pawed at his favorite blanket, digging the perfect sleep hole. Then he curled into a little ball, closed his eyes, and drifted off.

But just as his dreams carried him into a land filled with treasure, Wally heard a loud grunt. He was jolted awake. His left eye popped open.

He pricked his ears. Though he couldn't see in his dark cabin, Wally could hear something breathing very loudly.

And the *something* sounded close.

Wally's best friend, a boy named Henry, was asleep near Wally. The *something* snorted and snuffled. It sounded like something *big*. But Henry only giggled in his sleep, then rolled over.

Wally would have to handle this himself.

But what *was* this? It sounded like a monster with a stuffed-up nose. Wally gasped. Could there be a monster hidden under his bed? Wally nosed around the floor. He was careful not to get too close to the dark space under the bed.

Nothing smelled strange. The boards under his paws smelled like rats and other puppy pirates and scraps of leftover lunch. To Wally, the *Salty Bone* always smelled wonderful. The ship smelled like home.

The raspy breathing got louder and louder. The fur on the back of Wally's neck stood tall. He decided to wake Henry after all.

Wally put his paws on Henry's arm and licked his best friend's nose.

"Eh?" Henry muttered sleepily.

"Monster," Wally whispered. He pointed his paw toward the space below the bed. "Under there."

Henry's eyes got very wide. "In case you were wondering?" he whispered. "I don't like that sound. It's creepy." He tugged his blanket over his head.

The creature's breathing echoed in the dark cabin.

In, out, in, out.

"What could it be?" Henry said very quietly.

There was only one way to find out. Wally took a deep breath. He crouched and prepared to pounce. He poked his paw into the dark spaces in all the corners under the bed. His paw hit something hard. A baby rat squeaked and wiggled into a hole in the floorboards. Some dust and dirt scattered. Wally sneezed.

Henry lit the lantern. He held it so they could see under the bed. Both of them stared at the *something* making all that noise. Wally had always imagined monsters would be slimy. Or furry. With sharp claws and horrible breath.

This definitely didn't look like a monster.

It looked like a big cardboard cone with a long tube attached to it. Henry pulled it out to get a closer look. "What is this thing?" Henry asked, scratching his head.

Wally scrambled deeper under the bed to check things out. He noticed something else weird. There was a *hole* in the wall. If he looked through it, he could see straight through to Piggly and Puggly's quarters.

Wally pressed his eye to the hole. A pug's eye blinked back at him.

"You caught us!" Piggly barked, giggling. Wally backed away from the hole and a wrinkled pug snout nosed through it. Piggly's gold tooth glinted in the light from the lantern. "Ahoy, mateys."

Piggly and her twin sister, Puggly, squeezed through the hole. They squirmed out from under Wally's bed. Puggly sneezed. "We got you good with that pug prank!"

Wally had to admit it. They had fooled him. But how? "What is this thing?" he asked. He pointed to the funny cone and the strange tube.

"It's our monster maker!" Puggly told him. "When we breathe or talk into this tube, the sound travels through it and comes boomin' out the other end. Like monster sounds! Pug-glorious, eh?"

"We sure tricked you!" Piggly said. "Can't believe you thought there was a monster livin' under your bed."

"It sounded very spooky," Wally said. He put his mouth up to the tube and growled. His voice roared out of the cone. Wally sounded like a dog five times his size!

Henry tried it next. He cried "Yo ho ho" into the tube. The noise that came bursting out was so loud Wally had to cover his ears.

"That was a pretty good pug prank," Wally admitted.

"Oh, that's just the beginning of the prank," Piggly said. She and Puggly spun in happy circles. "Wait till you see what comes next!"

Don't Spook the Little Guy

"Puggly and I want to make everyone think there's a monster on our ship," Piggly said. "Want to watch?"

Henry and Wally looked at each other and grinned. Getting a little bit scared was kind of fun. Watching *other* pups get a little bit scared might be even more fun.

They followed the pugs toward the ship's kitchen, where the cook was hard at work.

Steak-Eye was whipping up a batch of his best stew. Unfortunately for the crew, Steak-Eye's *best* stew was some of the *worst* stew on all the seven seas. The cranky Chihuahua trotted back and forth across the countertop. He tossed a little of this and a little of that into a giant pot. His crazy tail whipped back and forth, knocking things off the counter and onto the floor. Steak-Eye muttered to himself as he worked, growling about nothing.

Wally and Henry hid behind a tall stack of boxes. They tried to stay very, very quiet as they watched Piggly and Puggly put their prank into action. The pugs tiptoed through the galley behind Steak-Eye's back. They shoved the megaphone under the kitchen counter. Then they dragged the long tube out into the hallway. The cook didn't notice a thing.

"Grrrrrr," Puggly growled into the monster

maker. The sound blasted out of the megaphone.

Steak-Eye nearly jumped out of his fuzzy skin. He slashed a stalk of celery back and forth like a sword. "Who's there?" he barked.

"*Arrrrrgh!*" Piggly roared next.

Steak-Eye jumped even higher this time. He landed on a pile of vegetables. Potatoes and carrots rolled every which way, scattering across the galley. Wally was filling up with giggles. He pressed his paw to his snout, but he couldn't hold them in. He burst into laughter. Before long, the pugs and Henry were laughing, too.

Steak-Eye whirled around. "Ya scurvy pugs," he growled.

"Gotcha!" laughed Piggly.

Steak-Eye lunged for her, but she was too quick for him. Piggly grabbed the monster maker and fled from the galley. Puggly, Henry, and Wally were hot on her heels.

They raced up to the deck, panting. That's when they spotted Spike napping near the front of the ship.

"Let's get Spike next," Puggly suggested. Spike, a chubby bulldog, was one of the biggest scaredy-dogs on the crew. He was afraid of almost everything.

Spike and his best friend, a tiny Boston terrier named Humphrey, were curled up in the sun. They were sharing Humphrey's small blanket. Wally watched nervously as the pugs set up the megaphone and got ready to roar again.

"*Arrr rarrr rarr rarr!*" Piggly barked into the tube.

Spike bolted upright. Humphrey barely moved.

"What's that?" Spike whined. When Puggly roared next, Spike threw himself on top of his tiny friend. "I'll protect you, Humphrey! No monsters are going to get my best mate."

"*Grunf,*" Humphrey squeaked. "Spike, you're crushin' me!"

Before Spike could smash his best friend, Piggly popped out of hiding. "Gotcha, Spikey!"

Spike and Humphrey both blinked at her, confused. "Eh?" Spike asked. "That sound came out of *you*?"

"Aye!" Puggly giggled. "Meet our new monster maker." She showed Spike and Humphrey how their megaphone worked. They wanted to try making monster sounds, too. So Spike and Humphrey joined the pugs, Wally, and Henry.

Next, they tried to surprise Millie and Stink. Millie and Stink, who called themselves the Weirdos, were the *Salty Bone*'s newest crewmates. They had spent years trying to trick other pirates into thinking their ship was a ghost ship, so they weren't easily fooled by funny noises. Neither of them was scared at all. But they both tagged along for the next prank.

"What about Einstein?" Piggly suggested. She lifted her snout to point at a small dachshund on the other side of the main deck. Einstein was studying a pile of maps, muttering quietly to himself.

"Sure," Puggly agreed, giggling.

Wally didn't know Einstein very well. The small wiener dog kept to himself most of the time. He was never picked for the captain's special projects, and he was never part of the crew who got to lift the sails or keep watch in the crow's nest.

Einstein padded toward the front of the ship and tripped on his own front paw.

"This is going to be fun," Piggly whispered.

The pugs set up the megaphone. Then the

whole group hid behind a stack of crates and watched as Henry yelled "Boo!" into the monster maker.

Einstein's ears pricked up when he heard the loud noise.

"*Ooga booga booga!*" Spike bellowed into the tube.

Einstein's eyes went wide. "Monster?" he

said quietly, looking around. "Monster!" He shrieked and put his paws up on the side rail, then looked down into the rolling ocean waves. "Sea monster!" he barked again. "Now what are the rules about sea monsters?" He squinted into the sky and blurted out, "Tell Captain Red Beard! I need to tell the captain we are under attack by a sea monster!"

Before anyone could tell him it was just a joke, Einstein raced across the deck on his stubby little legs. He slipped and slid a few times, but there was no stopping him.

"Uh-oh," said Puggly. "That little pup's gonna get us in *big* trouble."

Who Said Monster?

Wally, Henry, and the others chased after Einstein. Because he was small and narrow, Einstein was able to slip through spaces none of the others could. He reminded Wally of a fish slithering across the deck. He twisted and wiggled among piles of life jackets and the anchor and extra sails.

Puggly almost caught up with him . . . just as Einstein tripped in a puddle of water. He slipped, skidded, and slid down the deck—smack into Captain Red Beard. "Captain!" Einstein barked. The captain stumbled backward.

Einstein huffed and puffed. He was so nervous and out of breath that he choked on his words. "Sea gomster."

"What's that?" Captain Red Beard barked. He looked through Einstein like he wasn't even there. "Did someone say something?"

Piggly and Puggly both zoomed forward. "Nothin', sir."

The captain eyed the pugs. "Nothin', eh?"

Einstein jumped up and down. He pawed at the deck. But no matter what he did, Captain Red Beard didn't seem to notice. The gruff terrier turned away and went back to talking with his first mate, Curly.

Piggly and Puggly squeezed Einstein into a pug sandwich. Puggly whispered, "That was us, Einstein. Not a monster. We were playing a prank."

Einstein looked confused. "But I heard beastly sounds. *Ooga booga booga!*"

Spike looked embarrassed. "Uh, that was me."

"*You?*" Einstein growled. "*You* were trying to scare me?"

Spike nodded slowly.

"So what you're saying is, there is *not* a monster attacking us?" Einstein barked loudly. "I alerted the captain to a monster attack, and there *is no monster*?"

"Monster?" Captain Red Beard barked, spinning around. "Who said monster? Monster attack?!" Before the pups could answer, the captain sounded a loud horn. "Monster alert! Me crew, prepare for battle. We're being attacked by a monster!"

There was total chaos on deck as the crew ran to their stations and prepared to fight.

Spike yelped and dove under Humphrey's blanket. "A monster! Everyone hide!"

"Don't panic!" Wally barked loudly. But no one seemed to hear him. So Wally grabbed the monster maker from Puggly and shouted into it. "Avast! There is no monster!"

The pups all froze.

Captain Red Beard glared at Wally. “If I say there’s a monster, there’s a monster.”

“But, sir,” Wally began, “it was—” He stopped. He wanted to explain, but he didn’t want to get his friends in trouble.

Piggly lifted a paw into the air. “This was my fault, sir.”

Captain Red Beard growled. "Of course it was." Then he scratched his scruffy beard and said, "Monster or not . . . that was pretty exciting. Now I *want* to have a monster battle."

"But, sir, where are we supposed to find a monster?" Curly asked.

Captain Red Beard barked, "Maybe we should go on a monster hunt. Whaddya say, crew?"

Everyone but Spike cheered. Einstein jumped up and down, trying to get the captain's attention. "Ooh! Ooh! I have an idea of where we can search. I've been going over some maps, and I think— *Oof!*" He tripped and tumbled into a heap.

The captain stepped over him. "Who wants to set off on a pest for the great Sea Slug?" he asked the crew.

Curly leaned in and whispered, "Quest, sir. It's a quest—not a pest."

"That's right," the captain agreed. "We are going on a quest to find the slimy, horrible, great, and terrible Sea Slug!"

Old Salt coughed, and everyone quieted down. Whenever the wise old Bernese mountain dog had something to say, the whole crew stopped to listen. "Are you sure about this, Captain?" Old Salt asked.

"Sure as a shoe," said the captain.

"The Sea Slug is the most dangerous and angry beast in the sea," Old Salt told everyone. "No one has ever fought it and lived to tell the tale."

"So we'll be the first," Captain Red Beard boasted. "What better way to show those stinky kitten pirates who rules the sea!" He lifted a paw in the air and cheered, "Yo ho haroo. Puppy pirates, we are goin' on a monster hunt!"

Too Many Cats in the Sea

The puppy pirates sailed for many days and nights, searching for signs of the Sea Slug. The crewmates took turns on lookout duty. Every hour, a different pirate climbed up to the crow's nest and scanned the waves.

Einstein wanted a turn, too. But when he tried to climb the mast, the captain told him not to. "A clumsy pup like you would never make it to the top," he barked.

So Einstein stayed on deck. But he was still

eager to help. One morning, just after the sun had come up, Wally spotted Einstein peering through a spyglass. His ears were flat against his head. His tail stuck out like an arrow. He was scanning the horizon. "Ship!" he woofed suddenly. "There's another ship!"

Wally squinted into the distance. He couldn't see anything. But they were always supposed to tell Captain Red Beard about other ships. "Captain," Wally barked, "did you hear what Einstein said?"

"What? Who?" Captain Red Beard growled.

Before Wally could answer, Olly the beagle howled from up in the crow's nest.

"Einstein," Wally said. "He says there's a—"

"I don't have time for that pup's silliness," Captain Red Beard growled. "There's something afoot!"

"Ship!" Olly howled.

Henry bellowed, "Ship!"

"Did ya hear that? Ship!" Captain Red Beard barked.

Soon every pup on board was barking about the ship sailing toward them. Captain Red Beard snatched the spyglass out of Einstein's paws. Wally saw Einstein slink away. But Captain Red Beard didn't notice. He pressed his eye to the glass and peered out to sea. "Olly's right," he barked. "Shiver me timbers, I think it's the *Nine Lives.*"

"Kitten ship," Spike whined. "Hide!"

"Kitten ship?" Stink asked.

"What's the kitten ship?" Millie asked.

"The kitten pirates are our greatest enemies," Wally told Millie and Stink.

Henry scratched his head and said, "I wonder what the cats are doing in this part of the sea."

"Do you think the kitten pirates are on a monster hunt, too?" Curly asked.

"Only one way to find out," Captain Red Beard said. In his loudest voice, he yelled, "Avast, kitten pirates! What are you rapscallions up to?"

But the *Nine Lives* was too far away for the kitten pirates to hear him. "They're trying to yell something to us," Henry said. He craned his neck. "Nope. Can't hear a thing."

"Maybe we should send a message to the kitten ship in one of our dinghies," Einstein suggested. "I would be happy to row it over to them."

"Yeah," Piggly barked. "We need to get a message to the kitten pirates!"

Einstein's tail began to wag. Wally could see that he was excited about carrying a message to the kitten pirates. But Captain Red Beard had another idea.

"I like Piggly's plan. Wally and his boy can row a message over," the captain barked. "The human isn't good for much, but he does row like a champ."

"Maybe Einstein should come along, too,"

Wally said. "Since it was his idea?"

"Nonsense!" Curly laughed. "He'd fall out of the boat. Now off with you, so we can carry on with our monster hunt!"

Wally and Henry climbed into the dinghy. Henry rowed them through the gentle waves to the kitten ship. Two naughty Siamese kittens, Moopsy and Boopsy, were standing at the bow of the *Nine Lives.* Wally barked out a greeting. Henry glared at Ruby, the human girl who lived aboard the kitten ship.

Captain Lucinda the Loud said, "*Hiss!* What are you doing here, ya scurvy dogs?"

"We are searching for the mighty Sea Slug!" Wally barked back.

Captain Lucinda the Loud said, "Well, you tell your flea-filled captain we were here first. *We* are searching for the Sea Slug." The kitten pirate first mate, Paco the Claw, whispered

something to his captain. Lucinda the Loud hissed, "Nonsense, Paco. We can't let the puppy pirates *beat us*!"

Wally and Henry rowed back to the *Salty Bone* to deliver the kitten ship's message. Captain Red Beard was furious. He snarled, "Well, you tell Lucinda the Loud *we always win*!"

Henry and Wally rowed back and forth, delivering messages and threats between the two ships. The kittens refused to give up their quest for the giant Sea Slug. But the puppies weren't going to give up, either. So Captain Red Beard sent one last message to the kitten ship. "Walty, I want you to tell Lucinda the Loud and her crew this: It's a race! The first crew to find the Sea Slug wins!"

Slime Trail

The race was on!

The kitten pirates sailed east at top speed. The puppy pirates sailed west, as fast as they could. They all knew the Sea Slug lived somewhere nearby, but no one had any idea how to find the mysterious beast. The water was deep and dark in this part of the sea. If the Sea Slug didn't want to be found, they worried they would fail in their quest.

"Look over yonder," Wally said, putting his paws up on the starboard rail. "Land ho!"

Curly joined Wally. She peered out across the gold-tipped waves. "Shiver me timbers, it *is* land. Captain, let's stop and explore! Maybe we'll find a clue that will lead us to the Sea Slug."

The crew in the steering cabin nosed the ship toward the tiny island that jutted up out of the middle of the sea. Some crewmates hopped into dinghies and rowed toward land. Others leaped into the water and swam. The pugs blasted themselves to shore in their pug cannon. The cannon was something Piggly and Puggly had built. They used it to launch themselves into the air like hairy cannonballs. "Arrrr-*oooooo*!" Piggly cried as she sailed over the water.

"*Wheeeeee!*" Puggly cheered. She landed in a pile of rotten seaweed on the beach. Shaking herself off, she said, "Oof. Landing *still* stinks."

The island was small enough that they could explore it in less than an hour if they split into small groups. Everyone hustled to find partners. Spike and Humphrey stuck close to the captain. They wanted someone who could protect them if they came across anything creepy. Curly and Steak-Eye teamed up. Wally and Henry were always a pair, as were Millie and Stink. Before

long, everyone had formed groups. But Einstein still hadn't found anyone to be his partner. Everyone on board liked Einstein a lot. He just wasn't very good at running . . . or tracking . . . or swimming.

"Einstein, team up with us," Wally suggested. "Henry and I could use a few extra paws."

Einstein's face lit up. "Are you sure?"

"Aye," said Wally. The three of them set off along the seashell-filled shoreline. After they had only walked a short way across a small beach, they found a pile of wood blocking their path.

Henry raced forward to check it out. "In case you were wondering, mates? This is an old boat! It looks like something took a big bite out of it." He poked at the pile of broken wood with a stick.

"Do you think the Sea Slug tried to eat it?" Einstein wondered. He stepped onto one of the broken boards. But as soon as his feet scrambled up, he slipped back off. He tumbled into a hole, and Henry had to pull him out by the scruff of his neck.

"Careful, there," Henry warned. "Better watch your step."

Einstein hung his head. "Sorry."

"It's okay," Wally promised him. "Everyone slips."

"Not as much as I do," Einstein whispered. "Clumsy old Einstein. Always in the way. No help at all."

"Don't say that!" Wally told him. "You're a big help. Come on—let's keep exploring and you'll see."

The threesome continued their trek around the island. They were walking on shells, and the path was very slippery. "I wonder what makes these shells so slippery," Henry said. He picked one up and looked at it closely. He shrugged and kept moving.

As they made their way along the shoreline, they came upon another pile of wood every hundred paces or so. Each one was a broken boat that looked like it had a bite out of it!

"This is very strange," Einstein said. They

stopped beside a small fishing boat that was blocking the path. Wally and Henry scampered over the wreck, but Einstein was stuck. He couldn't go over, and he couldn't go under. "I'm going to go around this way, okay, mates?" He raced along the side of the ship, searching for some way past. He scrambled under bushes and around small trees.

As he waited on the other side, Wally could hear his crewmate yelping, "*Yow!*"

"Are you okay over there?" Wally called out.

"I'm okay," Einstein called. "Almost ther—*rooooo*!" His words turned into a howl.

Wally raced around the edge of the broken boat just in time to see Einstein slipping and sliding down a small hill. He rolled and tumbled. Then *splat!* He landed in a big, slimy puddle.

Einstein tried to scamper out of the puddle. But no matter how fast his feet worked, he kept

slipping back into it. Henry and Wally raced down the hill to help him. Together, they were able to pull the little dachshund out of the pool of slimy water. Einstein rolled around in a clump of grass to clean himself off. After a good roll, he was covered in dried-up grass but was no longer slimy.

"What *is* this stuff?" Henry asked. He scooped some of the slime into his palm and rubbed it between his fingers. "So slimy. Hmm . . ." He pulled his eyebrows together. Wally could tell the boy was thinking about something. "It may be crazy, but I have an idea."

Wally barked, "Tell us!"

"Could this be a puddle of Sea Slug slime?" Henry asked.

Einstein yapped happily. "Yes! I bet the great beast slimes things as she travels."

"Maybe that's why the shells along the shore are so slippery," Wally said.

Henry poked his finger into the slime again. "This stuff is pretty gross. I don't know if I want to find the monster that left this behind."

"We *have* to find it," Wally barked. "That's the whole point of a monster hunt." Now they knew the Sea Slug had been here. But how could they figure out where it went next?

"I know, I know!" Einstein jumped up and down. In his excitement, he slid into the slime—again. Wally and Henry pulled him out. "I know what to do!" Einstein yapped. "If we follow the trail of slime, we'll find the Sea Slug!"

The Search for Slime

Late in the afternoon, the crew gathered back on the small beach.

"Did anyone find something useful?" Captain Red Beard asked. "The kitten pirates must be hot on our tails. We can't let them catch us!"

Wally waited for Einstein to tell the captain what they had found. But Einstein didn't say anything. So Wally woofed to get everyone's attention. He told them about the puddle of slime. "Einstein thinks the Sea Slug leaves a trail of slime wherever she goes," he said. "If we can find slime in the sea, Einstein thinks we might find the beast."

"Great work, little Walty," Captain Red Beard said. He patted Wally on the top of his head.

Wally tried to explain. "Not me, sir. It was Einstein who—"

But the captain went on. "Did anyone else find anything?"

"Just a lot of scary leaves," Spike said in a shaky voice. "The leaves on this island look like *monster fingers*! So scary . . . and they tickled my ears."

No one else had found anything as interesting as the puddle of slime. So a few minutes later, the crew climbed back aboard the *Salty Bone* with their new clue. It was time to begin their search for slime.

"I could climb up to the crow's nest to look

for patches of slime on the water," Wally offered. Wally didn't like being in the crow's nest at the top of the mast. It was the highest part of the ship, just a tiny platform that seemed to float above the main deck. The wind was very strong, and Wally worried about getting blown away. But he knew the best way to get over his fear was to face it head-on.

"Climb, little Walty, climb!" Captain Red Beard barked. "We have to beat those pesky kittens to the Sea Slug. The race is on!"

Wally ran toward the rope ladder and dashed up, up, up. He settled in on the platform in the crow's nest. Squinting against the whipping wind, Wally searched the sea around their ship.

Though the wind was strong, the waves were small. The ocean was filled with strips of emerald green water that faded to the brightest blue. Far off in the distance, Wally thought he saw a section of water that looked black. Could it be slime? He wasn't sure, but it was worth checking out.

"Head east!" he called to the others. But when he peered at the deck far below him, he realized that no one could hear his barks. The wind was

too loud. He raced back down the rope ladder. Panting, he repeated his order. "Head east."

"Aye, aye, Slime Captain Wally," giggled Piggly. She was munching on a sausage, curled up on one corner of Humphrey's tiny blanket. Nearby, Puggly was kicking black booties off her paws, trying to make them land in a bucket. Henry was playing the fiddle, and a few puppy pirates were dancing along with the music.

Wally wished he could relax and play with his friends. Piggly's sausage sure smelled good! And playing games with Puggly was always fun. But he had a job to do. Slime Captain Wally! He liked the sound of that. Wally raced back to the top of the mast. When they reached the area where he thought he'd seen black in the water, Wally called, "Aye, I think it is slime. It curls up ahead and goes north."

Wally shouted out the information as loud

as he could. But it was no use. No one heard him. So he scrambled down the ladder again and repeated himself. The captain ordered the ship to head north.

Before Wally could race up the mast again, Einstein caught him and said, "Wally, maybe it would be easier if you had some help getting your messages to the crew. You can't keep running up and down to tell us what you're seeing."

Wally nodded. "The problem is, no one can hear what I'm saying from way up there. It's too windy."

"I know." Einstein squirmed around excitedly. "I have an idea. What if we put a few pups on the ladder? One can be near the top, close to you. One can be in the middle of the ladder. And another can be near the bottom, close to the captain and the rest of the crew." Einstein looked embarrassed when he said, "Maybe I could be the pup near the bottom of the ladder? Olly and Millie are great at climbing, so they can help, too. You can pass your message on to Olly, who will yell to Millie, who can pass it down to me. Then I can get the message to the captain."

"That's a great idea, Einstein," said Wally. Wally shared the idea with Captain Red Beard. He made sure he gave Einstein all the credit.

"Sounds like an interesting plan," Captain Red Beard said. "But I want Stink to be the pup at the bottom of the ladder. Einstein will fall off."

Wally glanced at Einstein. He looked very sad. "Please, sir," begged Wally. "Can he just try? It was his idea, after all."

"Oh, all right," Captain Red Beard agreed. Wally ran up the ladder first and got comfortable in the crow's nest. He grabbed a spyglass

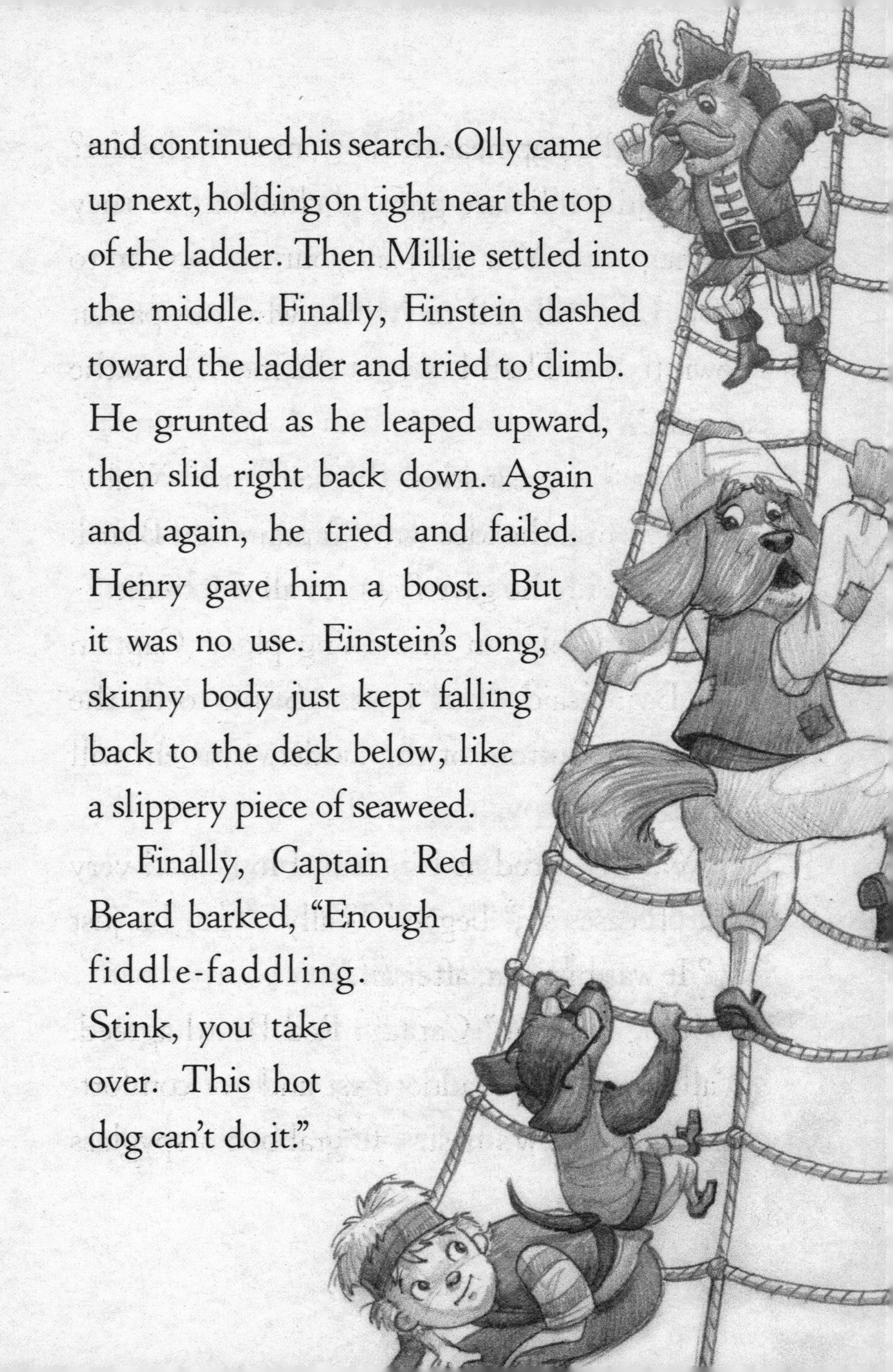

and continued his search. Olly came up next, holding on tight near the top of the ladder. Then Millie settled into the middle. Finally, Einstein dashed toward the ladder and tried to climb. He grunted as he leaped upward, then slid right back down. Again and again, he tried and failed. Henry gave him a boost. But it was no use. Einstein's long, skinny body just kept falling back to the deck below, like a slippery piece of seaweed.

Finally, Captain Red Beard barked, "Enough fiddle-faddling. Stink, you take over. This hot dog can't do it."

Einstein hung his head low.

When everyone was in place, the message train worked perfectly. Wally barked his directions to Olly, who yapped to Millie, who howled down to Stink. The ship zigzagged through the sea. Wally spun around in the crow's nest, searching the sea behind them. Far off in the distance, he saw a small dot. He knew it was the kitten ship. He wondered if they were following the same trail.

Wally spun around again and focused his spyglass on a patch of inky black water ahead. Through his spyglass, Wally could see the blackest part of the sea was beginning to bubble and froth.

The water below the *Salty Bone* churned with creatures. They were swimming away from the bubbling water as fast as they could. Big fish, small fish, eels, stingrays, and sharks zoomed past the puppy pirate ship at full speed.

Wally gulped. Only one thing could be so scary that even *sharks* would swim away. He took a deep breath and shouted, "Sea Slug!"

The Sea Slug

Wally climbed back down to the deck. The crew lowered the ship's sails so they could approach the bubbling water slowly.

"Prepare for battle!" Captain Red Beard hollered.

"Ready the cannons!" Curly barked.

"Keep Einstein away from the slime!" Piggly giggled. "He might fall in."

Einstein hung his head even lower. He whimpered.

"That was a good idea you had," Wally told Einstein. They were both up in the bow, paws propped on the front rail. The water around the ship was a beautiful blue, swirled with black slime. There was nothing to do now but wait for the monster to show itself.

"Really?" Einstein cocked his head. "Thanks."

"I would have had to run down from the crow's nest about a hundred times if you hadn't come up with that message train," Wally said. "So how big do you think the Sea Slug is? As big as our ship?"

Einstein shook his head, and his silky ears fanned out around him. "I don't know," he said. "But I guess I won't ever find out. It seems like I should just hide out in my quarters until the race is over, eh?" He hopped down from the rail.

"Why do you say that?" Wally asked.

"Because I won't be any help with the battle. And I might slip or trip or fall and ruin everything for everyone." The little dachshund sighed.

"Can I ask you something?" Wally said, sitting beside Einstein.

"Aye," Einstein answered.

"Why did you become a puppy pirate?" Wally asked.

Einstein flopped down and put his head on his front paws. "Pirating is in my blood," he said. "My family has always lived on ships. They're all rough and tough and fast—not me. But I always wanted to be a pirate! It's all I ever wanted to be! My family thought I wasn't cut out for it. I joined this crew to prove them wrong." He hung his head and added, "But maybe they were right. I'm not very good at climbing or sailing or fighting. I'm not very good at any pirate-y things. Maybe I don't have what it takes. Maybe I should quit."

Wally opened his mouth to tell Einstein not to give up. But before he could speak, a horn sounded. Wally peeked over the edge of the rail and saw that they had nearly reached the bubbling water.

"Crew!" bellowed Captain Red Beard. "We did it. We found the Sea Slug!"

"Hiss!" cried a voice. "*We* found the Sea Slug first!"

Wally looked over the port side rail. The kitten pirates had caught up to them!

"Neener nanner noo noo!" teased the kitten ship captain, Lucinda the Loud. "We won!"

"No, *we* won!" argued Captain Red Beard. The two captains yelled back and forth at each other for several minutes.

"We beat you!"

"No, *we* beat *you*!"

"Admit you lost, ya scurvy dogs."

"You cheated, furballs. You *followed* us."

Finally, Old Salt stepped forward. "Let's call it a tie," he said. "This is not the time to fight like cats and dogs."

The water below them had begun to bubble even more. As the crews from both pirate ships watched, something dark rose toward the ocean's surface. The water frothed. Even more slime filled the space between the two ships. A tentacle shot out of the water. It was greenish-black, with small yellow spots along one side.

"Sea Slug!" screeched Spike. "Hide me!"

The rest of the Sea Slug rose to the surface. Everyone grew silent. It was . . . small. *Very* small. It flicked a tentacle, and a spray of water hit the *Salty Bone*. Then it splashed at the *Nine Lives*. The kitten pirates screeched and ran for cover.

"In case you were wondering?" Henry said.

He was watching the Sea Slug slither through the water between their two ships. "That's not much of a beast. It's barely even the size of a Saint Bernard."

"Huh," said Captain Red Beard. "I would have thought the legendary Sea Slug would be bigger than that."

Even Old Salt looked surprised.

The kitten pirates hissed and murmured. Captain Lucinda the Loud swished her fluffy tail and said, "This won't be much of a fight."

"Not much of a fight at all," agreed Captain Red Beard. "A waste of time, really."

The two pirate ship captains stared each other down. "If we can't fight the Sea Slug," Captain Red Beard said finally, "maybe we should fight each other."

"Kitten pirates, prepare for battle!" shouted

Lucinda the Loud. Moopsy and Boopsy launched a hair ball at the *Salty Bone.*

"Puppy pirates, en garde!" barked Captain Red Beard. The pugs filled their cannon with water and blasted a shot at the *Nine Lives.*

The battle was under way!

But before either ship could launch a second attack, something very big rocked the water around them. Both boats lurched to the side. The tiny Sea Slug moved away as a second creature surfaced. This creature was also greenish-black with yellow spots. But it was not small. In fact, it was larger than the *Salty Bone*!

A giant plume of water blasted both ships, and out of the ocean rose . . . the real Sea Slug!

The Battle Begins

"Whoa," gasped Henry as the beast burst out of the water. The giant Sea Slug grew larger by the second. "That thing is bigger than a blue whale! In case you were wondering, blue whales are the biggest creatures in the sea. Their tongues weigh more than an elephant and—"

Captain Red Beard cut him off. "Enough talk," he barked. "We need a plan."

"*Two* Sea Slugs?" moaned Spike. He was

shaking with fear. "The first one was bad enough. This one could eat our ship whole!"

"Why do you think one of the Sea Slugs is so much smaller than the other?" Henry wondered aloud. He peered over the edge of the ship's rail. The enormous beast let out a loud groan and pushed the small Sea Slug under the water. The puppies and kittens all backed away from the edge of their ships. The smaller Sea Slug poked out of the water and squeaked, as if to answer the other.

"The little one actually seems kind of cute, now that we've seen the big one," noted Piggly. "That giant Sea Slug? Not as cute."

"Do you think the little one could be a baby?" asked Einstein. His voice was so small, though, that only Wally heard him. "And maybe the big one is its mama?"

Before Wally could tell him to say it again,

the giant Sea Slug bellowed loudly. Then she blew out a trail of slime that covered the ship's deck.

On Captain Red Beard's orders, Piggly and Puggly blasted the Sea Slug with water from the cannon. Curly and some of the quickest fighters stood with their swords ready. But the puppy pirates' weapons were no match for the Sea Slug. The water just rolled off its slippery back. The swords looked like silly toys next to

the giant beast. Everyone could see they were in a losing battle.

Over and over again, the Sea Slug rose out of the waves. It blasted slime and water at the two ships. Meanwhile, the smaller Sea Slug swam around and around the two pirate ships. The little creature swam so fast that the ocean water became a whirlpool. The *Salty Bone* and the *Nine Lives* spun around and around each other like they were caught up in a watery tornado.

Suddenly, a hair ball plopped onto the deck of the *Salty Bone.* "Well, shiver me timbers," snarled Captain Red Beard. "How can those frisky felines attack us at a time like this?"

Einstein plodded across the deck to inspect the hair ball. "Sir?" Einstein said, nosing the hair ball toward the captain. "This isn't a regular hair ball. This hair ball has a message inside it."

"A message?" gasped Curly.

"A message!" said Puggly.

"By golly, there's a message inside this hair ball," announced Captain Red Beard. He pawed the hair ball open and stared at the tiny slip of paper that was inside it. "This makes absotootly no sense at all! It's mumbo jumbo. Count on those foolish kitten pirates to waste our time during the most important battle of our pirating lives!"

"Captain, maybe it's some kind of code,"

Curly suggested. "Or a riddle. I bet Lucinda the Loud doesn't want the Sea Slug to intercept her message."

Henry stepped forward and read aloud from the paper. "'How do we get this battle done? One plus one equals won.'" He scratched his head. "They spelled *one* wrong. And that's bad math. One plus one is *two.* Even a kitten should know that!"

Curly looked confused. Old Salt thumped his peg leg against the deck. The puppies were stumped. All except for one. "I think I know what Captain Lucinda the Loud is trying to say," said Einstein. "She's asking if we want to team up to fight the Sea Slug."

Captain Red Beard looked down at Einstein. He studied him carefully, as if he had never noticed him before. "What's that you say, pup?"

"I said, I think the kitten pirates are

suggesting we work together. One plus one—their crew plus our crew—to win the battle." Einstein stepped back and added, "Sir."

Captain Red Beard growled. "*Team up* with

the kitten pirates? Never. No member of my crew would ever suggest such a thing. Traitor!"

"Einstein didn't suggest it," Wally said nervously. "He's just telling us what the message means."

Old Salt barked for attention. "And it's not a bad idea, is it?"

Everyone stared at him.

"We are fightin' a losing battle here, pups," Old Salt coughed. "If we work with the kitten ship, we might stand half a chance. But fightin' alone? We're doomed." He cocked his head. "Your call, Captain. But I know what I would do if I were in charge."

"Well then, *tell* us!" barked Captain Red Beard. "*What* would you do?"

"I just told you," said Old Salt with a sigh. "I'd team up. But this is your ship and your fight. You have to decide."

Not Tough Enough

After scratching his ears for a long time, Captain Red Beard decided that working with the kitten pirates was better than losing the battle. "What we need to do is plan our shots so we're all hittin' the Sea Slug at the same time," he told his crew. "They shoot, and we shoot. A one-two blast. The Sea Slug won't know what hit her. But how are we gonna get that message over to the kitten ship?"

"We could send a message in a bottle," suggested Spike.

"Or we could send a message with a Piggly," Puggly said. "I can blast her over to their ship with our pug cannon."

"What?" squealed Piggly.

"Someone's gotta go," said Puggly. "We can't row over in a dinghy. The Sea Slug might eat us. And it's only Piggly and me who can get shot outta the pug cannon." She turned to her sister. "So it's either me or you. And I've already been on the *Nine Lives*. I'm not going back."

"Fine," grumbled Piggly. "I'll be the hero. After I've told the kitten pirates our plan, I'll give you a signal. Three loud howls. *Arrrr-arrrr-arrrr-oooo! Arrrr-arrrr-arrrr-oooo! Arrrr-arrrr-arrrr-oooo!* On that signal, you fire your weapons. Got it?"

"Got it!" the puppy pirates all cheered.

Piggly climbed into the pug cannon. She

and Puggly had built it together, and usually the launch was only used for fun. Today it had a much more important purpose. With a loud *pop!* Puggly shot her sister up, up, and away. The chubby pug sailed through the air.

She flew over the Sea Slug.

Over the baby Sea Slug.

Over the black and blue sea.

Plop! It was a perfect shot. Piggly landed on the deck of the kitten ship and rolled. Through a spyglass, Wally could see his curly-tailed friend talking with Captain Lucinda the Loud. A moment later, they heard it:

Arrrr-arrrr-arrrr-oooo! Arrrr-arrrr-arrrr-oooo! Arrrr-arrrr-arrrr-oooo!

It was their signal to shoot. Right on cue, both ships launched their weapons. Hit from two sides, the Sea Slug roared up. Then she dropped down into the water. But a moment later, she shot up out of the ocean again. One tentacle flapped into the air, then pounded down. It just missed the bow of the *Nine Lives.*

Piggly howled and howled. The two ships took aim and fired. Water blasted from the *Salty Bone.* Hair balls flew at the Sea Slug from the *Nine Lives.* Hit twice more, the Sea Slug slipped

below the surface again. But the next time the slimy creature burst out of the waves, she was angrier than ever.

Over and over, the puppy pirates and the kitten pirates blasted the beast. Again and again, she fought back. Meanwhile, the smaller Sea Slug continued to splash both boats, trying to help. But the big Sea Slug kept nudging the little one out of the way. It seemed the big beast wanted to fight her own battle.

With the cats and dogs working together, the war against the Sea Slug felt more evenly matched. But even their combined power wasn't enough to win. The Sea Slug was just too powerful.

Wally saw that Einstein was trying to get Captain Red Beard's attention. But as usual, the captain didn't notice. "Einstein," Wally said, plodding over to him. "What is it?"

Einstein watched as another round of fire was blasted off the edge of the ship. "I—um—I have an idea," he said, watching the water closely. "It's probably a bad one."

"Your ideas are never bad!" Wally told him. "And we could use any idea—bad *or* good—right about now."

"No, I should probably just stay out of it. I don't want to bother anyone." Einstein shook his head sadly. "No one will listen to me anyway. They know I'm no good at being a pirate."

"Come on, Einstein," Wally urged. "You've been a great pirate all day. Your ideas are what make you great! We're fighting a losing battle with the Sea Slug. What do you have to lose?"

Wally glanced at Old Salt. The big Bernese mountain dog was listening to their conversation. Old Salt gave Wally a small nod. This made Wally feel like he was giving Einstein the right advice.

Einstein spoke softly when he said, "But my idea isn't a very *pirate* idea."

Old Salt cleared his throat and spoke up. "Is it a *good* idea?"

"Well . . . I think so," Einstein admitted. "But—"

"No buts. If it's a good idea, then it's a pirate idea," Old Salt said. He sounded very certain. "Running and climbing and fighting aren't what make you a good pirate, Einstein. If you're a pirate here"—he tapped his head—"and here"—he pressed his paw to his heart—"then you're a pirate where it counts. Some pirates are tough, some are brave, some are big, some are strong—and some are smart. There's not only one way to be a pirate, Einstein. You just have to find the way that's right for you."

Wally nodded. Old Salt was right. Every pirate on board had his or her own way of being a good pirate. Curly solved problems. The pugs played pranks. Henry wasn't even a *puppy*—but he was still a great puppy pirate. They were all different.

"Even if you don't run or climb or dig like a pirate, Einstein, you *think* like a pirate," Wally said. "That's just as important."

Einstein wagged his tail. "Really?"

"Really," Wally promised. He barked to get everyone's attention. "Puppy pirates, listen up! Einstein has something to say. And I think it's time we listened to him."

Little Einstein's Big Idea

Einstein stepped in front of the crew. He was shaking. Wally smiled at him and nodded. Einstein took a deep breath. He faced the other puppy pirates and said, "I have an idea." His voice was still as soft as ever.

"Eh?" Captain Red Beard growled. "Speak up if you want to be heard, pup."

Einstein raised his voice as high as he could and blurted out, "Just because the Sea Slug looks like a monster doesn't mean she *is* a monster."

"What's that?" Captain Red Beard interrupted with a laugh. "Are you tryin' to say that the greatest beast in the sea is *nice*? Have you seen her attackin' us? She's big and slimy, and she keeps blasting us." He shook his head and muttered, "That's a foolish thing to say, I tell ya. Foolish."

Wally was about to tell the captain to give Einstein a chance, but Einstein did it himself.

"Just hear me out, sir." He gulped. "Sure, the Sea Slug is big and slimy. And she looks really scary with her tentacles flapping around in the air. But it doesn't seem like she's trying to hurt us. I think she *could* hurt us if she wanted to. But instead she's just splashing and sliming us." Einstein trailed off, then said more quietly, "It almost seems like she's trying to keep us away from the little Sea Slug. Is it possible that she's just trying to protect her baby from an attack?"

"Her *baby*?" Spike whispered.

A few other members of the crew nodded. "He might be right," said Puggly. "The little one seemed like it was trying to play with us."

"And then we started a battle with the kitten ship," Wally added. "It probably seemed like we were attacking the baby Sea Slug."

"It's an interesting idea," Curly said. "So what do you think we should do, Einstein?"

Einstein's voice was shaking. "If we could somehow tell the Sea Slug that we don't want to hurt her baby, maybe she would let us go."

"But we're in the middle of a battle!" Captain Red Beard barked. "Are you sayin' we should surrender?"

Old Salt coughed. "It's important to pick your battles," he said. "Maybe this isn't the time or place for us to battle a great sea monster, eh?"

The crew all nodded.

"Fine," said Captain Red Beard. His shoulders slumped. "But how are we supposed to tell the Sea Slug that we're calling a truce? She's never gonna hear us over her own roaring. And we need to tell the kitten ship to stop fighting, too."

But Wally had already thought of an answer for that. He glanced at Puggly. "Remember how the pugs' monster maker made our voices really loud? What if we made an even *bigger* megaphone, one that will make our voices boom out over the sea?"

Everyone agreed that this was a great idea. The whole crew got to work right away, creating a huge megaphone out of wooden planks. They attached a long tube for hollering. When it was ready, a crew of pups held the megaphone up. Everyone agreed that Einstein should be the one to shout their message to the Sea Slug.

"Ahoy!" Einstein barked into the tube. "Sea Slug!"

The Sea Slug froze. It slowly turned toward their ship.

Einstein's tiny voice roared out of the huge megaphone. "Kitten pirates, hold your fire!"

The kitten pirates stopped blasting hair balls into the water. As soon as they did, the Sea Slug stopped shooting slime.

"Sea Slug!" Einstein shouted. "We want to call a truce."

The Sea Slug slithered through the waves toward the *Salty Bone.* But she still wasn't shooting slime at them. Wally thought that was a good sign.

"We don't want to hurt you or your baby." Einstein looked back at the rest of the crew. They all

nodded, urging him to keep talking. "We will sail away and leave you alone. We only ask that you do the same."

Everyone on board both ships held their breath. Seconds passed. Neither the kitten pirates nor the puppy pirates fired any more weapons. Finally, the enormous Sea Slug wrapped one tentacle around the tiny Sea Slug's body, and both creatures disappeared under the waves. The ocean was calm once again.

"Hip hip hooray!" cheered the puppy pirates.

When they were sure it was safe, Wally and Henry rowed over to the *Nine Lives* to pick up Piggly and bring her back to the ship. Puggly cheered when she found out her sister had snuck a pot full of the kittens' stew back to the *Salty Bone* under her coat.

"Three cheers for Einstein!" Captain Red Beard said, giving Einstein a friendly nudge.

"But what did I do?" Einstein asked, confused, as the crew started cheering for him.

"It takes one smart pirate to keep a cool head in battle," Captain Red Beard said. "Thinking creatively and speaking up take real bravery. I think I owe you an apology, Einstein. We're lucky to have a pup like you on our crew."

Einstein beamed. Wally's tail wagged. He was happy for his friend. And happy that the ship didn't get eaten by a sea monster!

Soon the *Salty Bone* was sailing toward the sunset. The puppy pirates were curled up on the deck, tired after the chase and their battle. They all relaxed and snacked while Henry played them a few songs on his fiddle.

"We do have one problem now," said Captain Red Beard.

“What’s that, Captain?” asked Curly.

Captain Red Beard scratched his chin. “I’ve been searching for the Sea Slug all my life, Curly,” he said. “And today we discovered the legendary monster isn’t much of a monster after all. . . . Well, what are we supposed to do now?” He sighed. “Pirates always need a great beast to search for.”

“There’s always the Terrible Ten-Tentacle Squid,” Puggly reminded him.

“And the Thousand-Year-Old Snippy-Snappy Turtle,” added Steak-Eye.

“Don’t forget about the Snarling Shark of the Seven Seas!” barked Olly.

“Someday the baby Sea Slug will be all grown up,” Old Salt pointed out.

Spike whined and stuffed his nose under Humphrey’s blanket. Wally thought of all the strange creatures out there and shivered. It was a little scary—and a lot exciting. He wondered what their next adventure might be. He had a feeling he wouldn't have to wait very long to find out.

"Well," said Einstein, "until we find the next sea monster, this will have to do." Everyone laughed when he pulled out Piggly and Puggly's monster maker and barked, "*Ooga booga booga!*"

All paws on deck!

A Super Special Puppy Pirates
is on the horizon.
Here's a sneak peek at

Best in Class

"Show dog training," Henry announced, after reading the sign on the door. The group walked inside to get a closer look. Dozens of dogs stood in a neat circle around the outside of the room.

All the dogs looked like they had taken a bath that very day. Some pups had little bows in their fur, like Puggly often wore, and others had haircuts that must have taken hours! But the strangest thing was that the class was almost completely silent, and no one was moving.

Wally and the others waited for something to happen. But the dogs just kept standing there.

And standing there.

Finally, after what felt like a hundred hours, the lead dog stepped into the center of the ring. He trotted slowly around the room in a perfect circle. One by one, each of the students took a turn doing the same thing. It was the most boring thing the puppy pirates had ever seen.

Puggly was the most bored. She yawned. Then she started sniffing around the edges of the classroom. She nosed open a box filled with ribbons. "Loot!" she woofed. The other puppy pirates surrounded her. Puggly hopped inside the box and buried herself under hundreds of different-colored ribbons.

Henry rustled around at the bottom of the box. He pulled out a big gold medal. He studied the front of the medal. "Best in Class," he said, reading the words. He draped the medal over his own chest and laughed. "Look, mates! I won Best in Class at puppy school."

Once Puggly had played inside the box of ribbons for a while, she continued her search for fun. She tipped over a box of toys, spilled a pail of treats, and then nosed open a chest filled with tiny dog tutus. "Lookie here, Piggly!" she whispered. "This is the kind of show dog *I* like to watch!" She whipped off her cape and booties and wiggled into one of the frilly skirts. She balanced on her hind legs, jumped in circles, and giggled as the tutu fanned out around her smushy belly. "Hey, show dogs!" she barked. "It's showtime!"

New friends. New adventures. Find a new series . . . just for you!